The Children's Picture Prehistory
EARLY MAN

Anne McCord
Illustrated by Bob Hersey
Designed by Graham Round

Series Editor Lisa Watts
Consultant Editor Professor M. H. Day

Contents

Assistant Editor Tamasin Cressey
Additional artwork by Joe McEwan

Anne McCord is a lecturer in the Education
Section of the British Museum (Natural History).
Michael H. Day is Professor of Anatomy at
St Thomas's Hospital Medical School, London
University, London, England.
First published in 1977 by Usborne Publishing Ltd
20 Garrick Street, London WC2E 9BJ, England.
2nd printing 1978
3rd printing 1979
Copyright © 1977 Usborne Publishing Ltd
Published in Canada by Hayes Publishing Ltd,
Burlington, Ontario.

Printed in Belgium by Henri Proost & Cie pvba.

The Story of Man

Like all the other animals on the Earth today, man slowly developed from prehistoric animals which lived long ago. The first people lived about three million years ago. For hundreds of thousands of years, they lived in caves, hunted for their food and made tools from stones and antlers.

These pictures take you back through the story of man to the animals which were our earliest ancestors. These lived about 150 million years ago at the same time as dinosaurs.

Today, most of our food is grown by farmers with machines to help them sow and harvest the crops. Early people hunted for their food. They did not know how to farm.

People learned how to plant seeds and grow crops about 11,000 years ago. They collected the crop by hand and cut it with sickles which had flint blades.

About 350,000 years ago, people first learned how to make fire and use it to cook and keep warm. The earliest people were probably afraid of fire.

The first people lived about three million years ago. They learned how to make rough tools from stones by chipping them to give sharp edges.

About 14 million years ago there were no people on Earth. Monkey-like creatures, which were ancestors of man, lived in the trees and ate fruit.

About 150 million years ago, giant scaly-skinned reptiles called dinosaurs lived on the Earth. The earliest ancestors of people were small hairy creatures which hid in trees to escape the dinosaurs.

Man's Relatives

Man belongs to the same group of animals as monkeys, chimpanzees and gorillas. This group is called the primates. Primates are mammals, that is, animals which have hairy skin, give birth to babies and feed them with their milk.

All the primates developed from small, prehistoric primates which lived in the trees about 65 million years ago. Here are some modern primates.

40 cm long

Modern tree shrews look like the first prehistoric primates. They eat insects and live in trees in Asia.

120 cm long

Lemurs are found only on the island of Madagascar. This is a ring-tailed lemur.

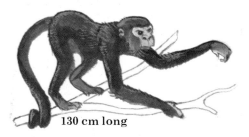
130 cm long

Spider monkeys live in the tallest trees in the forest and can grip with their tails. They live in South America.

about 1 m long

Baboons are another kind of monkey. They live together in troops and are found in Africa.

120–150 cm tall

Chimpanzees belong to the family of apes. They are more closely related to man than the other primates. They live in Africa.

Primates' special features

The primates developed so that they could survive in the trees. They have hands which can grip branches and good eyesight for judging distances.

People inherited these features from their monkey-like ancestors. Man has good eyesight and hands which can grip tools.

Bushbaby

The long fingers and toes of primates can curl round and grip branches. No other animals have hands and feet like those of the primates.

Gorilla

Primates see a separate picture with each of their eyes. Their brains put the two pictures together. This is called stereoscopic vision.

Test for stereoscopic vision

You can try this test for stereoscopic vision to see how it helps you to judge distances.

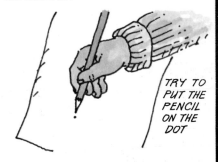
TRY TO PUT THE PENCIL ON THE DOT

Mark a dot on a piece of paper and stand about 60 cm away from it. Close one eye and try to put the point of a pencil on the dot without hesitating. Try with the other eye and then see how much easier it is with both your eyes open.

Early Primates

Animals change, very slowly, over millions of years and become quite different. This is called evolution. We know about evolution because the remains of prehistoric animals have been found buried in the rocks. These remains are called fossils.

People who study fossils and find out about prehistoric animals are called palaeontologists. They have found very few fossils of man's early ancestors, but they think that prehistoric primates called *Ramapithecus** were our direct ancestors.

Man's ancestor

Fossil teeth

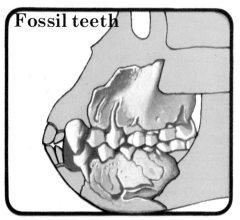

This is part of the fossil jaw of *Ramapithecus*. The jaw and teeth are shaped more like a human's than an ape's and scientists think it was an ancestor of man.

Ramapithecus lived in the trees in forests between six and 14 million years ago. They were about the size of monkeys and were probably good climbers.

At some stage, man's ancestors began to live on the ground and walk on two legs. *Ramapithecus* may sometimes have climbed down from the trees and run across the ground.

1 How fossils were made

When an animal died, it was sometimes covered with layers of mud and sand or with lava from a volcano. Its flesh rotted away, leaving its skull, bones and teeth.

2

Very, very slowly the mud and sand or lava hardened to form rock. The skull, bones and teeth were preserved in the rock. They are the fossils that are found today.

When they lived

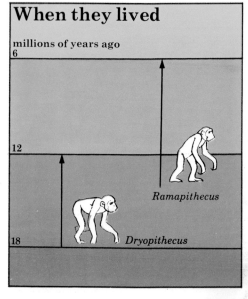

millions of years ago
6

12

Ramapithecus

18

Dryopithecus

Prehistoric ape

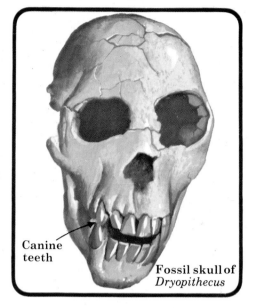

Canine teeth

Fossil skull of *Dryopithecus*

This is a prehistoric primate called *Dryopithecus*. Scientists think it may have been the ancestor of modern apes because it had long, ape-like canine teeth.

Dryopithecus lived in forests around 14 million years ago. The skull of *Dryopithecus* shown on the right was slightly crushed as it became fossilized.

Clues from teeth

The shape of the fossil jaws of *Ramapithecus* show that it was related to man. The sides of the jaws slope outwards, like man's. The jaws of *Dryopithecus* are more like those of a modern ape and have straight sides.

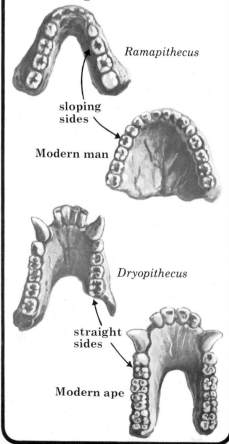

Ramapithecus

sloping sides

Modern man

Dryopithecus

straight sides

Modern ape

What is evolution?

In the animal world, only the strongest, fittest animals which are best adapted to their surroundings can survive. The weaker animals die out.

If the surroundings change, animals which have different qualities may be better adapted to the new surroundings. These animals will survive and have babies like themselves. The other animals will gradually die out. This is how animals evolve and become quite different.

As the primates evolved, some of them adapted to live in the treetops, some in the middle branches and others on the ground.

Chimpanzees live on the ground and in the trees and are good climbers.

Colobus monkeys can climb and jump safely in the highest branches.

Baboons live on the ground. The fierce males defend the troop from attack by leopards.

The Near-Men

About three million years ago creatures we call hominids were living on the grassy plains in Africa. The name hominid comes from the Latin word *homo*, which means man.

There were two different kinds of hominids living at that time. One of them was a direct ancestor of man and is called *Homo*. The other is called *Australopithecus*. There were several different kinds of *Australopithecus*. The hominids probably could not talk and had not yet become people.

Australopithecus robustus lived together in small groups. They were about 150 cm tall and were strong with big muscles and long ape-like arms.

They had large teeth and strong jaws for chewing tough plants. The brain of *Australopithecus* was about half the size of modern man's brain.

Fossil skulls of hominids

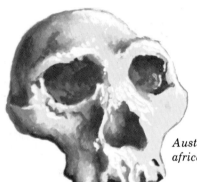

Australopithecus africanus

Like the other early hominids, *Australopithecus africanus* had a thick ridge of bone above his eyes. His brain case was small.

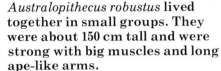
Australopithecus boisei

This is the fossil skull of *Australopithecus boisei*, another kind of *Australopithecus*. He had very large jaws and a ridge of bone on top of his head.

Life on the plains

Australopithecus and *Homo* probably lived together in the same place. They could live in the same area because they ate different kinds of food.

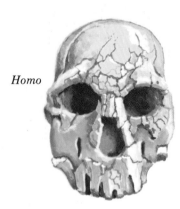
Homo

Homo had a larger brain than *Australopithecus* and so his skull was rounder on top. When the skull was put together, missing pieces were filled in with blue plaster.

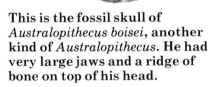
When they lived

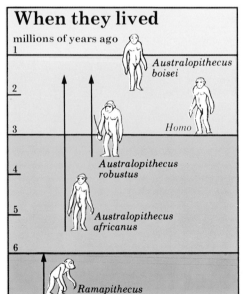

millions of years ago

1

Australopithecus boisei

2

Homo

3

Australopithecus robustus

4

Australopithecus africanus

5

6

Ramapithecus

2

Australopithecus africanus were only about 120 cm tall. They had smaller teeth than *robustus* and ate meat which is easier to digest and needs less chewing than plants.

They caught small animals to eat. They probably used branches or stones to kill their prey and to defend themselves from other animals on the plains.

Fossil sites in Africa

AFRICA

Hadar •

Lake Turkana • Koobi Fora

Lake Victoria • Olduvai Gorge

All the fossils of these hominids were found in South and East Africa.

•• Sterkfontein

Swartkrans

Small groups of *Homo* probably hunted animals to eat. Stone tools over $2\frac{1}{2}$ millions years old have been found, but palaeontologists do not know which hominid made them.

Australopithecus robustus ate berries, leaves and fruits. They did not know how to store food and had to move around to find enough to eat every day.

They may have pushed twigs into a termites' nest to pull out the small white grubs and eat them. Modern chimpanzees eat termites like this.

Australopithecus robustus probably dug up roots with sticks and took birds eggs and ate them raw. Palaeontologists do not know if they made tools or not.

The First People

About $1\frac{3}{4}$ million years ago, small groups of people lived by the side of a lake in East Africa. These people were our direct ancestors. They are called *Homo habilis*, which means "handy man". *Homo habilis* made rough stone tools from pebbles.

Since the time when *Homo habilis* was alive, a river has cut a deep valley through the land. This valley is called Olduvai Gorge. Fossil remains of both *Homo habilis* and *Australopithecus* have been found at Olduvai.

Stone tool

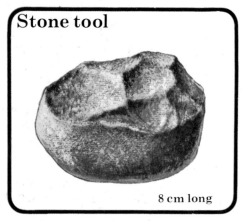

8 cm long

This is a stone chopper which was made by *Homo habilis*. It is about $1\frac{3}{4}$ million years old and was found in Olduvai Gorge. *Homo habilis* cut meat with it.

Life at Olduvai

Homo habilis built shelters of branches to protect them from animals and cold winds.

The children probably played and fought as children do today.

The men went hunting and brought their kill back to the camp to share with the others.

1 Going hunting

Homo habilis had a larger brain than *Australopithecus*, and was more intelligent and skilful. They worked together to hunt animals to feed their group.

2

The hunters had no weapons and probably crept up on their prey and then pounced on it. They killed it with stones, or with heavy branches.

3

Stone tools were heavy to carry around, so they were probably made on the spot. The hunters used sharp flakes of stone to cut up the meat to carry it home.

Volcanoes near the lake sometimes erupted and bones were preserved as fossils in the lava.

The women stayed near the camp with the children. They collected eggs, berries and small animals to eat.

Homo habilis was about 1½ m tall

Homo habilis made stone tools by chipping pebbles to give them sharp edges.

If they killed an animal near the camp, the women and children may have run up to share the meat. They ate it raw because they did not know how to make fire.

Palaeontologists have found fossil animal bones which had been cracked open. These show that early people broke open the bones to eat the soft marrow inside.

Make an early man mask

You will need some newspaper, a paper bag, a water-based glue such as wallpaper paste and some wool and paints.

1

BAG STUFFED WITH NEWSPAPER

Mix the glue with water to make a thin paste. Stuff the paper bag with crumpled newspaper and tear the rest of the paper into pieces about the size of your hand.

2

COVER ONE SIDE ONLY

Wet pieces of newspaper in the glue and then paste them flat on to the paper bag. Cover one side of the bag with gluey paper, building it out in the middle.

3

EYE-BROW RIDGE

SIDE VIEW

Mould a nose, lips and eyebrow ridge from lumps of gluey paper. Stick them on to the newspaper on the paper bag and cover with smooth pieces of gluey paper.

4

HOLE FOR STRING

When the newspaper is dry, pull out the paper bag. Then paint the mask and glue on some wool for hair. Pierce two holes for eyes and two holes for the string.

The Fire Makers

Very slowly, as thousands of years went by, the early people evolved and changed. By about a million years ago they were taller and had larger brains than their ancestors.

These people walked upright without stooping and are called *Homo erectus*. They lived between about 1½ million and ¼ million years ago. Fossils of their remains have been found near fire-blackened hearths in caves. These show that by about 300,000 years ago, *Homo erectus* had learned how to make and use fire.

Hunting with fire

Homo erectus frightened animals into an ambush with flaming branches. They caught them with a weapon called a bolas.

The early hominids were terrified by natural fires in the grasslands. The heat, smoke and noise frightened them as it did the other animals.

Gradually the early people learned not to be afraid of fire. They probably took advantage of other animals' fear and caught them as they ran away from the flames.

Homo erectus was about 1½ m tall.

A bolas was made of three round stones wrapped in pieces of skin and tied together with leather thongs. Flung by a hunter, it wrapped round an animal's legs so it fell down.

When they lived

years ago
250,000

1 million

Homo erectus

2 million

Homo habilis

Australopithecus

The camp fire

Fires helped *Homo erectus* survive in cold weather. His fossil remains have been found in northern China, where the weather was quite cool.

At first *Homo erectus* used fire, but did not know how to make it. They may have taken flaming branches from a forest fire and carried them back to their camp.

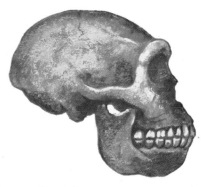

With a fire alight in their cave, *Homo erectus* had light and warmth at night. They may have sat around the fire and told hunting stories or made stone tools.

Homo erectus probably noticed that animals which had been burnt in fires were easier to eat than raw meat. So they began to throw meat on the fire to cook it.

Comparing skulls

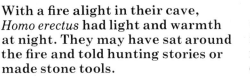

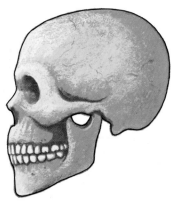

The skull of *Homo erectus* was smaller than that of modern man and like earlier hominids, it had a thick ridge of bone above the eyes and no chin.

Modern man's skull has a high forehead and pointed chin. The forehead and chin of *Homo erectus* sloped backwards and his brain case was smaller than ours.

Could early people talk?

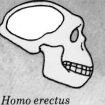

Homo erectus   Modern man

Homo erectus had larger brains than those of earlier hominids, but still not as large as ours. Earlier hominids could not speak, but *Homo erectus* probably grunted sounds and simple words to talk to each other.

A Camp on the Beach

The first *Homo erectus* lived in Africa, but gradually they spread to other parts of the world. A camp site where early people lived over 350,000 years ago has been found in Nice, a town on the south coast of France.

Palaeontologists called this camp site *Terra Amata*, after the street in Nice where it was found. They think a band of *Homo erectus* hunters visited the site every year. They stayed there for only a few days at a time while they hunted animals such as elephants and rhinos.

Wandering hunters

During the year, the band of hunters and their families moved from place to place, following herds of animals. They visited *Terra Amata* in late spring.

Yellow broom flowers in late spring. Palaeontologists found fossil pollen from these flowers in the camp and this shows the time of year when it was built.

Fossil footprint

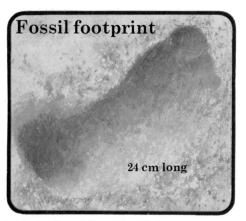

24 cm long

This is the oldest fossil footprint of a human being. A man or woman must have slipped and left a deep heel mark in the mud about 350,000 years ago.

Elephants and rhinos came to drink from the river.

The women probably collected shellfish from the beach and did not go far from the camp.

At *Terra Amata*, palaeontologists found the remains of a wooden hut about nine metres long and five metres wide. They also found stone tools and fossil animal bones.

The early people built the hut from branches with two wooden posts to hold up the roof. There were large rocks beside the hut to protect it from the wind.

Lighting the fire

They probably still did not know how to make fire. They may have carried hot ashes from their old camp fire and used them to light the fire in the new camp.

Near the fire there was a kitchen area where food was prepared and cooked. The people were very untidy and left rubbish and animal bones in the hut.

Prehistoric hearth

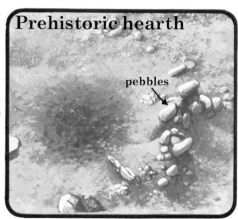

pebbles

This is the hearth where the people lit their fire. They put pebbles round the fire to shield it from the wind and the heat baked and darkened the sand.

Today the sea level is lower and the site of the camp is in the town, not on the beach.

They hunted elephants and rhinos and the deer and fierce wild boars which lived in the forest.

The camp had to be near a fresh water spring because the people had nothing to carry water in.

The people slept on skins near a fire which was kept burning inside the hut. There was also a flat stone where someone sat to make stone tools.

The men went off to hunt animals for the group to eat. They knew that elephants and rhinos came to drink from the river near the camp.

They collected driftwood from the beach to burn on the fire.

Where *Homo erectus* lived

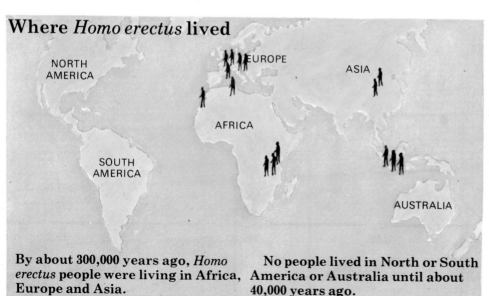

By about 300,000 years ago, *Homo erectus* people were living in Africa, Europe and Asia.

No people lived in North or South America or Australia until about 40,000 years ago.

Was early man hairy?

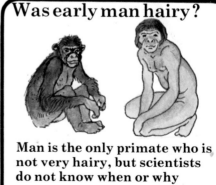

Man is the only primate who is not very hairy, but scientists do not know when or why people become less hairy.

One result of this is that human mothers have to carry their babies in their arms. Ape babies can cling to their mothers' hair.

An Elephant Hunt

By about half a million years ago, early people had become skilful hunters. Fossils found near a village called Ambrona, in Spain are proof that an elephant hunt took place there about 300,000 years ago.

On this site, palaeontologists found stone tools and the fossil bones of butchered animals. There were also traces of charcoal which showed that fire had been used to frighten the elephants into an ambush. For such a large hunt, several bands of hunters probably joined forces.

The hunters knew that at a certain time every year, a herd of elephants passed through this valley in search of new pastures. So they lay in wait for them.

When they saw the elephants, the men set fire to the grass on the hillsides. The elephants were terrified of the fire and stampeded down the valley.

3 The kill

The more the heavy elephants struggled in the marsh, the deeper they sank in the thick mud. Some of them collapsed, exhausted and the hunters killed them by stabbing them with their pointed wooden spears.

The hunters used tools called hand-axes to cut up the animals. A hand-axe was a stone which was sharpened at one end and held in the palm of the hand.

They probably ate the soft brains and liver of the animal straight away. Then they cut off the rest of the meat and took it back to the camp to cook.

Palaeontologists found an elephant's fossil leg bones and tusk laid in a line. They think the hunters used them as stepping-stones in the wet marsh.

The elephants' escape was blocked by marshy land. With the hunters yelling behind them and fire on either side, the frightened animals rushed into the marsh.

1 Digging up the evidence

Workmen discovered the fossil elephant bones when they were digging a trench. Later palaeontologists visited the site and began to excavate it.

First they used stakes and string to divide the area into squares. Then, very carefully, they removed the earth from each square.

2

They sieved every spadeful of soil to make sure that no evidence was thrown away.

3

Fossil bones and tools were left in place until they had been mapped, numbered and photographed.

4

The fossils were wrapped in plaster to protect them while they were taken to the laboratory.

5

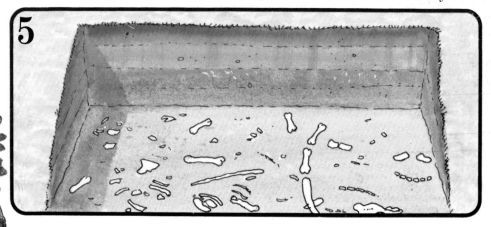

When the diggers had removed all the earth, they found fossil elephant bones, stone hand-axes and charcoal from the fires. There were no human fossils.

The fossil tusk and leg bones which the hunters probably used as a bridge, were in a line across the site. Tests on the soil proved that it had been marshy.

Stone Age Tools

About 2½ million years ago, people first learned how to chip stones to give them sharp cutting edges. These sharpened stones were early man's first tools.

The time when early man lived is called the Palaeolithic Age, which means "Old Stone Age". During this time people made all their tools from stones, bones, wood or antlers. The oldest known tools are called pebble tools. They were very rough but early people gradually became more skilful.

1 Making a tool

First the hunter had to choose a rock. He knew which kinds of rocks made the best tools and sometimes went a long way from the camp looking for good rocks.

2

He used a round pebble as a hammerstone to hit the rock. By carefully aiming his blows he could shape the tool the way he wanted.

Man's special grip

Man can touch his thumb with his middle and index finger. This is called the precision grip. Chimpanzees and other primates can only clench their hands in the power grip.

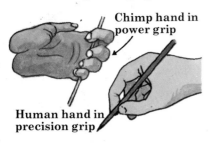

Chimp hand in power grip

Human hand in precision grip

With the precision grip, man can hold things between his fingers. This enables him to make and use fine tools.

Chimps sometimes make and use very simple tools. They pull the leaves off twigs and use them to hook grubs out of termites' nests.

The story of tools

The early hand-axes were used for lots of different jobs. Later people made different tools for special purposes and stopped making hand-axes.

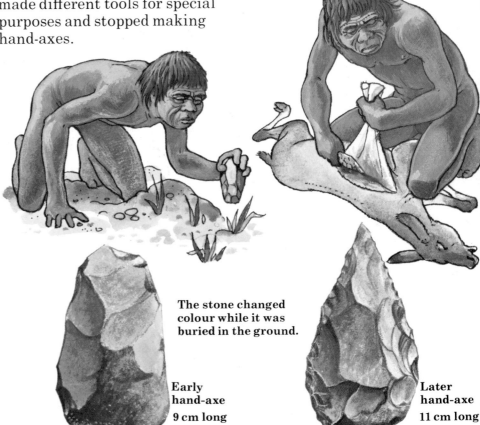

The stone changed colour while it was buried in the ground.

Early hand-axe 9 cm long

Later hand-axe 11 cm long

About a million years ago, people made large hand-axes with blunt ends. The edges were not very finely flaked and these tools were used for digging and for cutting up animals.

This sharp-edged hand-axe was made about 300,000 years ago. Its edges were very finely flaked. It was used for stripping the skins off animals and for cutting and scraping meat from bones.

3 The tool maker knocked several large chips off the rock to make the rough shape of the tool. If the rock broke in the wrong place he had to start again.

4 Next he used an animal's bone as a hammer to chip small flakes from the edge of the rock. This gave the tool a very thin, sharp edge. The flakes were used to cut meat.

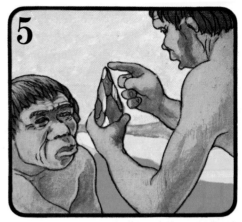

5 The finished tool is called a hand-axe. It had a pointed end, a thin cutting edge and a rounded base which was held in the palm of the hand.

Scraper
5 cm long

Gradually, early people learned how to shape flakes of rock into different kinds of tools. This is a tool called a hollow scraper which was used to sharpen sticks to make spears.

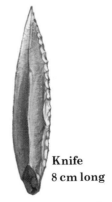

Knife
8 cm long

About 40,000 years ago, people made sharp, knife-like blades from flakes of rock. They also made chisel-like tools called burins for shaping needles or spearheads from antler.

Tool time chart

This chart shows when some of the different kinds of Stone Age tools were made.

years ago
10,000

 Blades

50,000

Later hand-axes

200,000

Early hand-axes

1 million

 Choppers

 Pebble tools

2½ million

The Palaeolithic, or Old Stone Age, lasted from 2½ million years ago until 10,000 years ago. About 40,000 years ago, people stopped making hand-axes and made all their tools from flakes of rock.

Neanderthal Man

By about 250,000 years ago, *Homo erectus* had evolved and changed and become a new kind of people. These new people are included in the same group as modern man and are called *Homo sapiens*.

In the past there were several different kinds of *Homo sapiens*, but today there is only one. One of the early kinds of *Homo sapiens* is called Neanderthal man. Neanderthal people lived during the ice age, about 50,000 years ago, when large parts of the world were covered with ice.

Hunting in the ice age

Neanderthal people were short and stocky with large muscles. They were very strong and were the first people to adapt to living in in very cold places.

The people hunted animals such as woolly mammoths with wooden spears. They ate its meat and used its skin and thick shaggy hair to keep them warm.

Neanderthal skull

The skulls of Neanderthal people had thick brow ridges and large teeth. The backs were pointed but the brains were the same size as modern man's brain.

Tools

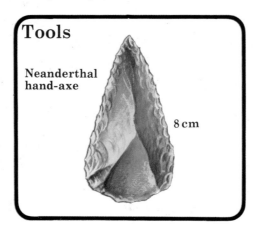

Neanderthal hand-axe

8 cm

Neanderthal people were skilful at making tools. Their hand-axes were smaller and easier to manage than those of earlier people such as *Homo erectus*.

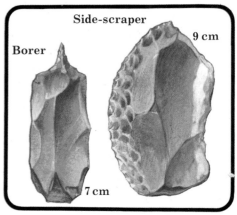

Side-scraper

Borer

9 cm

7 cm

They made stone scrapers for cleaning the fat from animal skins and borers for making holes. The scraper had a round edge for scraping and a straight edge to hold.

Cooking

Neanderthal people may have cooked meat on flat stones. First they lit a fire on the stones to heat them.

When the stones were hot the fire was swept away and the meat was thrown onto the hot stones.

The heat from the stones slowly roasted the meat. This made it tender and easier to chew.

1 Model cave

You will need a paper bag, some newspaper, water-based glue, such as wallpaper paste, and plasticine and paints.

DIP PAPER IN GLUE

Stuff the paper bag with newspaper and cover one side of it with pieces of newspaper soaked in glue, as described on page 9. Leave it to dry for several hours.

A Neanderthal home

Neanderthal people lived in caves or built huts from branches covered with animal skins. Sometimes they built huts inside the damp, cold caves or in the shelter of an overhanging rock.

To make clothes from animal skins they first had to remove the fat from the inside of the skin. They pegged the skin taut on the ground and cleaned it with a stone scraper.

They may have dried the skins in smoke from the fire to keep them soft and leathery. Then they pierced holes in the edge of the skin with a pointed stone borer.

They probably wrapped themselves in the skins and threaded leather thongs through the holes to join the edges. They may have bound their feet in skins too.

2

TRIM WITH SCISSORS TO MAKE A STRAIGHT EDGE

When the newspaper is quite dry, pull out the paper bag to leave the hollow cave. You can paint the cave and put a cave painting inside like those on page 24.

3

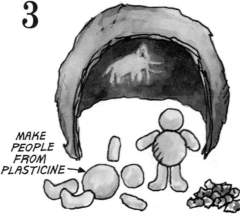

MAKE PEOPLE FROM PLASTICINE →

To make plasticine cave people, shape the body, legs, arms and head from plasticine and press them together. Stick bits of gravel in their hands as tools.

4

STICKY TAPE

GRAVEL

You could make a model fire from twigs and red paper and sprinkle earth on the cave floor. To make trees, tape some leafy twigs to the outside of the cave.

19

Cave Bear Magic

1

Neanderthal people hunted fierce cave bears. They believed that the bears' skulls and bones could make magic and probably thought this magic would keep them safe.

2

To catch the bear they followed its footprints back to the cave where it lived. It was a dangerous hunt because the bears were over $3\frac{1}{2}$ m long and very fierce.

3

They probably threw burning branches into the cave to smoke out the bear. The hunters waited outside with their wooden spears tipped with stone.

4

The angry bear came rushing out of the smoky cave and the hunters leapt at it with their spears. Others probably threw heavy rocks at the animal. Some of the men may have been killed in the fight.

5

When the bear was dead, they cut off its head and carried it back to their cave. They put the head in a pit with the skulls of bears killed in other hunts.

Magic skull

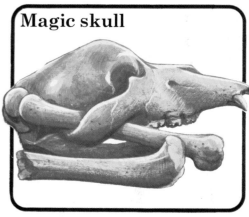

This skull of a cave bear was found in a cave where Neanderthal people lived. They had put the leg bone of a young bear into the skull of an older bear to make magic.

Burying the Dead

The first people spent most of their time hunting and collecting food. They probably never wondered how life began, or what happened to them when they died.

Neanderthal people seem to have been the first to bury their dead. Palaeontologists have found skeletons buried in graves in the earthy floors of caves where Neanderthal people lived. The bodies were sometimes buried with tools which perhaps they believed they would need in their next lives.

This is the entrance to a large cave in the mountains of Iraq. Inside, palaeontologists found the grave of a 40-year-old man who died about 60,000 years ago.

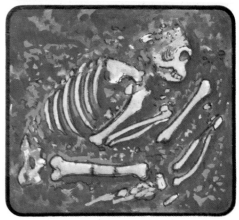

The man's bones were preserved as fossils by the weight of the earth on top of them. He had been laid curled-up in the grave with his knees under his chin.

It must have taken a long time to dig a hole in the earthy floor of the cave. The Neanderthal people had only pointed stone tools and sticks to dig with.

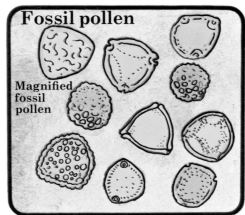

Fossil pollen

Magnified fossil pollen

Scientists found fossil pollen in the grave which showed that the man had been buried with flowers. This is what pollen looks like under a microscope.

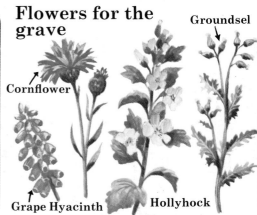

Flowers for the grave

Groundsel

Cornflower

Grape Hyacinth

Hollyhock

These are the kinds of wild flowers which were in the man's grave. They still grow in parts of Europe, so you may be able to find them.

The burial

The Neanderthal people laid the dead man on some pine branches and scattered wild flowers from the hills over his body.

The First Modern People

Neanderthal people died out about 40,000 years ago and a new kind of *Homo sapiens* evolved. These new people were the first to have the same shaped skulls and bodies as modern man. They are called the Cro-Magnon people and were our direct ancestors.

Cro-Magnon people lived in caves or huts towards the end of the last ice age. The weather was cold and snowy and only short grass and shrubs could grow. The people hunted reindeer and woolly mammoths.

1 Hunting and fishing

Cro-Magnon people made many new kinds of tools and weapons. They tied antler points, with barbs pointing backwards, on their spears to wound animals.

They used spear throwers to help them throw spears further. The spear throwers were carved from antler and some were decorated with carved patterns.

Sewing

Needles made from antler were found with the remains of Cro-Magnon people. This shows that they sewed skins.

Cro-Magnon people used a chisel-shaped stone tool called a burin to cut the antler. They were probably the first people to make needles and sew.

They bored a hole in the tip of the needle to make an eye. Then they smoothed the sides and point by rubbing the needle on a piece of stone.

They probably used a stone borer to make holes in the leather so they could push the needle through. They sewed with thin strips of leather or gut.

Cro-Magnon people often stitched little beads of coloured rock to their clothes to decorate them. Sometimes they used shells with holes in them too.

Ancient burial

Many graves of Cro-Magnon people have been found in the floors of huts and caves. This skeleton was covered with beads and shells from the clothes which had rotted away.

Cro-Magnon skull

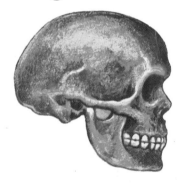

This is the skull of a Cro-Magnon woman. It is the same shape as skulls of modern people and has a large, rounded brain-case, a pointed chin and upright forehead.

They caught fish with harpoons which were carved from antlers and had backward-pointing barbs. They tied the harpoons on to spears and stabbed the fish with them.

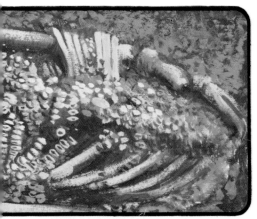

Bodies were often laid on their sides in the graves, with their knees pulled up to their chins. Sometimes there were tools and weapons in the graves too.

When they lived

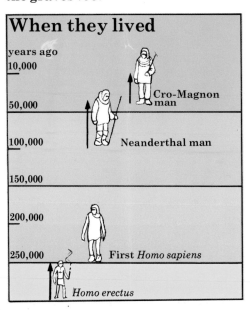

years ago
10,000

50,000   Cro-Magnon
                         man

100,000   Neanderthal man

150,000

200,000

250,000   First *Homo sapiens*

Homo erectus

Mammoth bone huts

Some Cro-Magnon people lived on the cold, flat steppe lands of eastern Europe. There were no caves to live in and few trees for wood to build huts. They hunted woolly mammoths which provided nearly everything they needed.

They built huts from mammoths' long leg bones and tusks, covered with skins. They stood the bones in skulls, because they could not push them into the frozen ground.

These Cro-Magnon people wore trousers and jackets made from mammoth skins. They ate mammoth meat and stored it in pits dug in the cold ground.

Make cave man's necklaces

Cro-Magnon people made necklaces from little stones and shells, fishbones or bits of eggshell. They probably threaded seeds and fruit pips too, but these have rotted away.

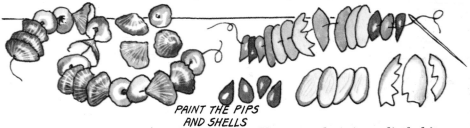

PAINT THE PIPS AND SHELLS

Sea-shells and stones often have little holes in them. If you visit the seaside you could collect them and thread them on thin string for a necklace.

You can also pierce little bits of fresh eggshell with a needle. Thread them on cotton to make a necklace with apple and orange pips.

Cave Painting

In the depths of their caves, Cro-Magnon people painted pictures of the animals they hunted. They were probably the first people to discover how to paint and use colour, though Neanderthal people may have decorated their bodies with a powdered red rock called ochre.

Cro-Magnon people may have painted the pictures to make magic. Perhaps they believed that the pictures would keep them safe and help them catch the animals they hunted for food.

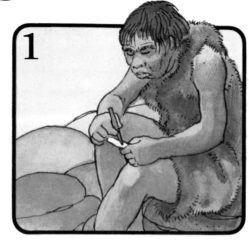

No remains have been found of pictures painted by earlier people. They probably painted and scratched patterns on bits of wood which have rotted away.

Cro-Magnon people painted pictures of horses, bison and reindeer. Often they put spears in the paintings as magic to make their own spears kill the real animals.

Magic carvings

Cro-Magnon people carved figures in stone of very fat or pregnant women. They also modelled statues in clay and dried them in the fire.

The people may have believed that carvings like this would bring them good fortune.

Painting the caves

Cave paintings by Cro-Magnon people have been found in France and Spain. The colours are still very bright, although they were painted over 30,000 years ago.

The early cave paintings were always of animals and hunting scenes, so it was probably the men who painted them.

They lit the cave with lamps made by burning fur or moss soaked in animal fat.

The paints were made from coloured soft rocks. They ground the rocks to a powder between a bone and a stone and mixed the powder with animal fat.

A Cro-Magnon artist put his hand on the rock and then blew paint round it through a reed. There are few pictures of people or plants in the early paintings.

This engraving on a rock wall shows a woolly mammoth with its long, shaggy hair. Cave art often shows us what the prehistoric animals looked like.

Make a cave painting

You will need some plaster of Paris, a box such as a large size matchbox, a piece of string, sticky tape and paints.

1

MAKE ENDS OF STRING STICK UP

STICKY TAPE

Take a bit of string about 6 cm long and fold it in half to make a loop. Tape the loop end of the string on to the bottom of the box on the inside.

2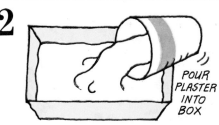

POUR PLASTER INTO BOX

Mix the plaster of Paris with water to make a thin paste and pour it into the box to make a layer about about 3 cm deep. Leave it to dry and then tear the box off the plaster.

3

Copy or trace one of the cave paintings on this page on to the slab of plaster. Then paint it, using the same colours as the cave men: red, yellow, brown and black.

4

CARVED LINES

You could also make a cave man's engraving. Copy the shape of the woolly mammoth in box three on to a plaster slab. Then carve the lines with an old fork.

> Sometimes they painted the outline of the animal first and then filled it in with moss or fur pads soaked in paint.

They stored the paint in hollow bones with lumps of fat in the ends. There was no green or blue paint as these colours were not found in the rocks.

The artists made brushes from animal hair tied to small bones. Sometimes they put the paint on with their fingers, or used little pads of fur or moss.

Hunters in the Forest

The ice age ended about 10,000 years ago and the weather became warmer. In northern Europe trees and forests grew again. The animals, such as mammoths and woolly rhinos which had lived during the ice age, died out. The people living then looked very like modern people.

At about this time, people in the Middle East learned how to plant seeds and to farm. In Europe they still hunted for their food and used bows and arrows for the first time.

Lakeside village

The remains of camps where hunters lived about 10,000 years ago have been found in Denmark and England.

Piles of broken tools, animal bones, fish bones and shells were found near the camp. These rubbish heaps are called middens.

The people hollowed out tree trunks with their axes to make boats. The remains of several boats have been found.

They shot ducks and other birds with arrows. They ate the meat and used the feathers on their arrows.

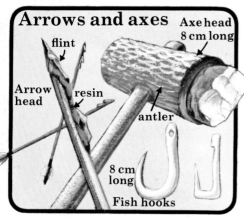

Arrows and axes

flint

Arrow head

resin

Axe head 8 cm long

antler

8 cm long

Fish hooks

The hunters made axes by fixing sharp, chipped stones into hollow antlers. These were joined to wooden handles. They chopped down trees with these axes.

People often camped near lakes in clearings in the forest. Where the ground was wet and muddy, they built their houses on platforms of tree trunks.

They cut down trees to build their houses and covered the branches with skins to keep out the rain. The ground was damp so they covered it with bark.

1 Going fishing

Remains of a fish trap about 1 m long

This is the remains of a fish trap which was found in a marsh in Denmark. The people ate lots of fish which they caught in traps, or with harpoons or hooks.

2 They made the fish trap from the long, thin branches of willow trees. They peeled the bark off the branches and wove them together in the shape of baskets.

3 To catch the fish the hunters built a dam across a stream. They put the trap in an opening in the dam. When the fish swam through they were caught in the trap.

The women collected fruits and berries from the forest.

The hunters had tame dogs to help them chase and kill wild animals.

Hunting in the forest was always difficult and dangerous. The men hunted red deer, roe deer and wild pigs. Bows and arrows were the best weapons to use in the forest.

The tips and barbs of arrows were tiny flakes of stone, glued on with resin. This is the sap from birch trees. Feathers balanced the arrows in flight.

Rock paintings

These paintings were done about 10,000 years ago in Spain. Unlike earlier paintings they show human figures. The man is shooting deer with a bow and arrow.

This is a rock painting of a woman collecting honey from a bees' nest in a tree. The bees are shown swarming angrily round their nest.

The first dogs

Dogs are descended from wolves. They probably first became tame when wolf cubs were caught by hunters and taken back to their camps. Wolves live in packs and the strongest wolf is its leader. If a wolf grows up amongst people it is obedient to its human master.

The First Farmers

In the Middle East, about 11,000 years ago, people discovered that they could sow the seeds of wild plants and grow the crops they needed.

These people were the first farmers. They planted wheat and looked after sheep and goats which had become tame. They had a constant supply of food and no longer had to move around the countryside, hunting animals and collecting plants to eat. They built villages near their land and settled down to farm it.

In the warm, dry lands of the Middle East, wheat grew wild on the hills. People collected the grain of the wheat as well as fruit and nuts to eat.

They carried the wheat back to their camp and ground it between two stones to make flour. Some of the wheat probably fell on the ground and grew near their huts.

The first farm animals

The wild ancestors of sheep, goats, pigs and cattle lived in the Middle East. They became the first farm animals.

The people hunted these animals and sometimes carried young lambs or goat kids back to the village.

The young animals became tame. Their babies were tame too and soon the village had a herd of animals.

The farmers looked after their herds and protected them from wild animals. They drank the milk from the animals and killed them when they wanted meat or skins. They no longer needed to hunt wild animals.

Farming village

The walls of the houses were made from a mixture of mud and straw which had dried and hardened in the sun. Rain damaged the walls and they had to be repaired after the winter. The roofs were thatched with straw covered with mud.

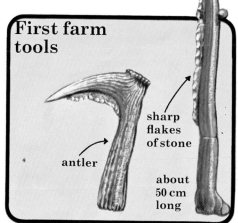

3 The people noticed that wheat plants grew from fallen seeds. They tried scattering seeds on land which they cleared near their camp and waited for plants to grow.

4 They collected the ripened wheat and had enough grain to last them for several months. They made tools, called sickles, for cutting the stalks of the wheat.

First farm tools

sharp flakes of stone

antler

about 50 cm long

The farmers' sickles were made from flakes of flint fixed in handles. The handles were made of wood or from the jaw bone or antler of an animal.

Some of the houses had several rooms and the floors were covered with mats woven from rushes. One of the buildings was a store house, or granary, for the wheat. In the courtyard of the houses there was a large oven which was built of dried mud.

Baking bread

In the yard outside the houses there was a large oven where the women baked bread. The oven was made of dried mud and a fire was lit inside.

The women ground the wheat to make coarse brown flour. They mixed the flour with water and shaped the dough into flat, round loaves. The loaves were baked on stones heated in the oven and the bread was thin and hard.

Time Chart

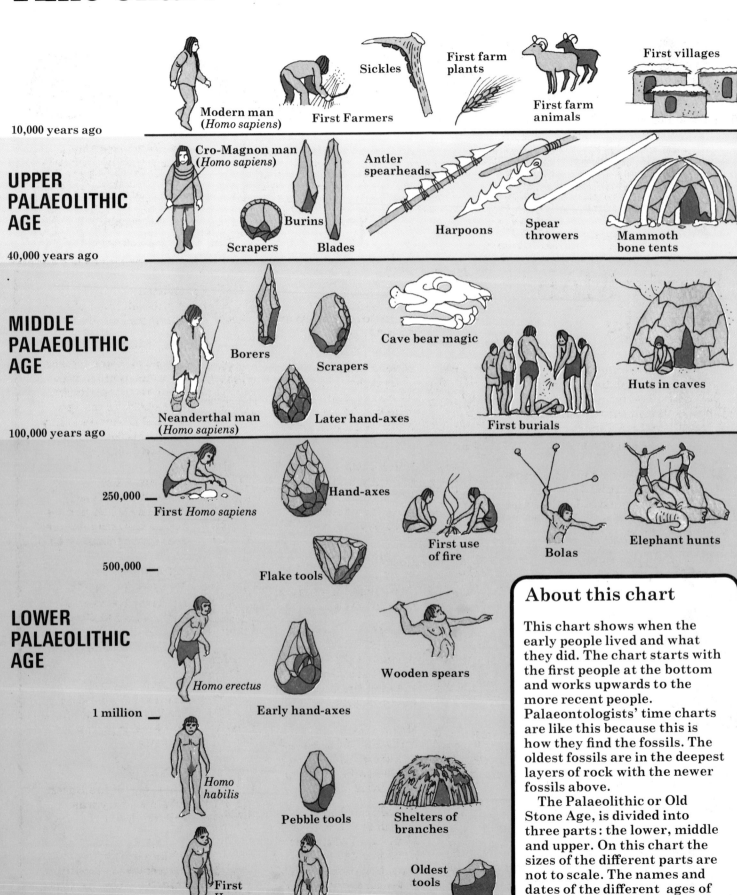

10,000 years ago — Modern man (*Homo sapiens*) · First Farmers · Sickles · First farm plants · First farm animals · First villages

UPPER PALAEOLITHIC AGE

40,000 years ago

Cro-Magnon man (*Homo sapiens*) · Scrapers · Burins · Blades · Antler spearheads · Harpoons · Spear throwers · Mammoth bone tents

MIDDLE PALAEOLITHIC AGE

100,000 years ago

Neanderthal man (*Homo sapiens*) · Borers · Scrapers · Later hand-axes · Cave bear magic · First burials · Huts in caves

250,000 — First *Homo sapiens* · Hand-axes · First use of fire · Bolas · Elephant hunts

500,000 — Flake tools

LOWER PALAEOLITHIC AGE

Homo erectus · Early hand-axes · Wooden spears

1 million — *Homo habilis* · Pebble tools · Shelters of branches

First *Homo* · *Australopithecus* · Oldest tools

2½ million years ago

About this chart

This chart shows when the early people lived and what they did. The chart starts with the first people at the bottom and works upwards to the more recent people. Palaeontologists' time charts are like this because this is how they find the fossils. The oldest fossils are in the deepest layers of rock with the newer fossils above.

The Palaeolithic or Old Stone Age, is divided into three parts: the lower, middle and upper. On this chart the sizes of the different parts are not to scale. The names and dates of the different ages of early man are at the side.

Hunters in Europe

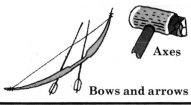

Bows and arrows

Axes

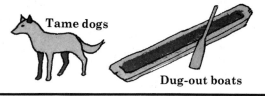

Tame dogs

Dug-out boats

Fish traps

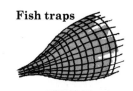

Cave paintings

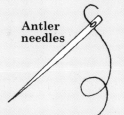

Carved figures

Antler needles

Jewellery

Sewn clothes

Early Man Words

Australopithecus
("Southern Ape")
The name of a group of man-like creatures whose fossils have been found in Africa.

Bolas
A hunting weapon made from round stones wrapped in leather and joined together with leather thongs.

Burin
A chisel-like tool made from a flake of stone.

Cro-Magnon man
A type of modern man who lived between 40,000 and 10,000 years ago.

Evolution
The way animals and plants slowly change over millions of years.

Fossils
Remains of ancient animals and plants preserved in the rocks.

Hand-axes
Tools made by chipping stones to give them sharp edges.

Hominids
The name for the ancestors and relatives of man.

Homo erectus
("Upright man")
The ancestors of man who lived between about a million and $\frac{1}{4}$ million years ago.

Homo habilis
("Handy man")
The ancestors of man who lived about $1\frac{3}{4}$ million years ago.

Homo sapiens
("Wise man")
The scientific name for modern man.

Ice age
Long period of time when the climate was very cold and large areas of the Earth were covered with ice.

Mammals
Animals which have fur or hair, give birth to babies and feed them with their milk.

Mesolithic Age
("Middle Stone Age")
The period of time in Europe from the end of the ice age, about 10,000 years ago, until people began to farm about 6,500 years ago.

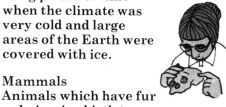

Midden
A rubbish heap of bones and shells.

Neanderthal man
A type of *Homo sapiens*, or modern man, who lived between 100,000 and 40,000 years ago. Named after the valley where his fossil bones were found.

Neolithic Age
("New Stone Age")
The time when people began to farm and use new types of stone tools.

Palaeolithic Age
("Old Stone Age")
The time between $2\frac{1}{2}$ million and 10,000 years ago when early people first made stone tools.

Palaeontologist
A scientist who studies fossils to find out about prehistoric plants or animals.

Prehistory
The story of the Earth before history was written down.

Primates
The group of mammals which includes lemurs, monkeys, apes and man.

Going Further

Finding fossils

If you find a stone that looks like a Stone Age tool, you could take or send it to your local museum. They will tell you if it really is a tool made by early man, or if it is a stone that has been worn down by rivers, wind and rain.

If you find old bones, the museum will identify these for you too, but they are fossils only if they are over 10,000 years old.

Books about early man

Fossil Man by Michael H. Day (Hamlyn)
All About Early Man by Anne McCord (Carousel)
Early Man by J. Kleibl (Hamlyn)
    The following books in the Time Life Emergence of Man series have good pictures of early man, stone tools and fossils:
The Missing Link
The First Men
Neanderthal Man
Cro-Magnon Man

Museums

The Natural History Museum, London England has a large collection of fossil skulls which show how early man evolved. In the British Museum, London, you can see Stone Age tools. There are also exhibitions about early man in museums in Oxford, Cambridge, Cardiff, Edinburgh and Glasgow.

In Australia, the National Museum of Victoria and the Australia Museum, Sydney have collections of prehistoric life.

Index

In this index the scientific names are written in *italics*. The English meanings of the Latin and Greek names are in brackets.

32